I'd Really Like to Eat a Child

I'd Really Like to Eat a Child

By Sylviane Donnio

Illustrated by Dorothée de Monfreid

Random House 🏠 New York

Every morning, Mama Crocodile would bring tasty bananas to little Achilles for his breakfast, and each time she said in wonder, "What a big boy you are getting to be, my son! And how handsome! And what beautiful teeth you have!"

"True," Achilles would say to himself.

But one morning, Achilles refused to eat. This worried Mama Crocodile.
"Don't you want a tasty banana for breakfast?" she asked.
"No thanks, Mom," Achilles answered. "Today, I'd really like to eat a child."
"What an idea, my little Achilles!" his mother cried. "Well, children don't
grow on banana trees, only bananas do, and *that's* what I have for breakfast!"

"I know, but I'd really like to eat a child!"

Papa Crocodile had an idea. He ran to the village and brought back a sausage as long as a truck for his son. "No thanks, Dad," Achilles answered. "Today, I'd really like to eat a child."

"Come now, Achilles. There's no such thing as a sausage made from children!"

"I don't care," snapped Achilles. "I want to eat a child!"

Luckily, Mama and Papa Crocodile were clever. "Our Achilles has a sweet tooth," they said. "Let's make him a big, yummy chocolate cake. Then he'll totally forget this silly idea."

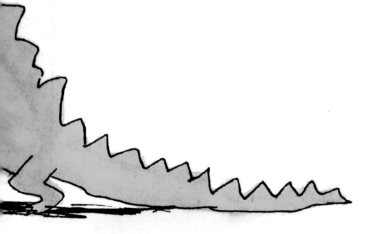

And that's just what they did.

The cake was magnificent. "WOW!" Achilles shouted when he saw it.
He picked out a great big piece. . . .

But then he sighed and changed his mind. "Nope," he said.
"Today, I'd really like to eat a child."

Mama and Papa Crocodile were beside themselves.
They cried and moaned, "Boo-hoo-hoo! What will we do?
Our dear Achilles won't eat!"

Achilles was beginning to feel strange and rather weak all over—
which is exactly what happens when you haven't eaten your breakfast.
    A nice swim would do me good, he thought. So he walked down to
the river.

There, on the riverbank, was a little girl playing by herself.
"Yippee! Finally, I'm going to eat a child," Achilles whispered to himself.
He crept up slowly and bared his beautiful teeth, like a
ferocious beast ready to pounce.

RAAH!

"Oh! Look at that," the little girl cried. "A teeny-tiny crocodile! He's awfully cute! And so scrawny! He must not eat very much."

As quick as a wink, the little girl caught Achilles by
the tail and tickled his belly. "Coochie-coochie-coo!"

Then, when she'd had enough, she threw him into the river.

Achilles emerged from the river hungrier than ever. "Darn! I blew it!"
he said. And he ran all the way home shouting, "Daddy, Mommy! Quick,
give me some bananas! I have to grow bigger . . ."

". . . *BIG* enough to eat a child!"

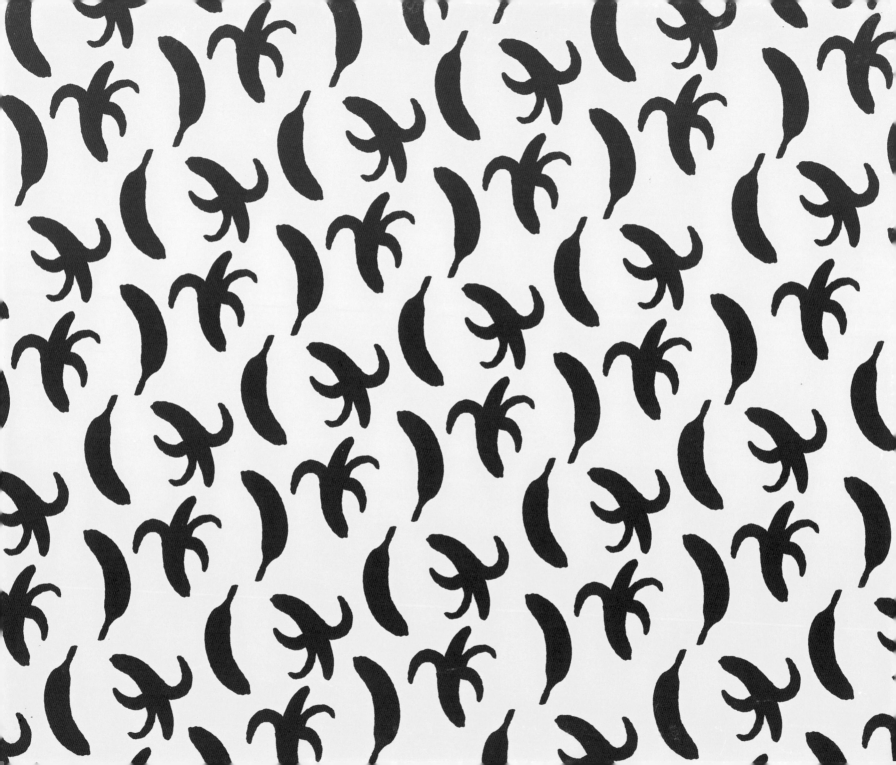